Dear mouse friends,
Welcome to the world of

Geronimo Stilton

The Editorial Staff of
The Rodent's Gazette

1. Linda Thinslice
2. Sweetie Cheesetriangle
3. Ratella Redfur
4. Soya Mousehao
5. Cheesita de la Pampa
6. Coco Chocamouse
7. Mouseanna Mousetti
8. Patty Plumprat
9. Tina Spicytail
10. William Shortpaws
11. Valerie Vole
12. Trap Stilton
13. Dolly Fastpaws
14. Zeppola Zap
15. Merenguita Gingermouse
16. Shorty Tao
17. Baby Tao
18. Gigi Gogo
19. Teddy von Muffler
20. Thea Stilton
21. Erronea Misprint
22. Pinky Pick
23. Ya-ya O'Cheddar
24. Ratsy O'Shea
25. Geronimo Stilton
26. Benjamin Stilton
27. Briette Finerat
28. Raclette Finerat
29. Mousella MacMouser
30. Kreamy O'Cheddar
31. Blasco Tabasco
32. Toffie Sugarsweet
33. Tylerat Truemouse
34. Larry Keys
35. Michael Mouse

Geronimo Stilton
A learned and brainy
mouse; editor of
The Rodent's Gazette

Thea Stilton
Geronimo's sister and
special correspondent at
The Rodent's Gazette

Trap Stilton
An awful joker;
Geronimo's cousin and
owner of the store
Cheap Junk for Less

Benjamin Stilton
A sweet and loving
nine-year-old mouse;
Geronimo's favorite
nephew

Geronimo Stilton

VALENTINE'S DAY DISASTER

Scholastic Inc.

New York   Toronto   London   Auckland   Sydney
Mexico City   New Delhi   Hong Kong   Buenos Aires

If you purchased this book without a cover, you should be aware that this book is stolen property. It was reported as "unsold and destroyed" to the publisher, and neither the author nor the publisher has received any payment for this "stripped book."

No part of this publication may be reproduced, or stored in a retrieval system, or transmitted in any form or by any means, electronic, mechanical, photocopying, recording, or otherwise, without written permission of the publisher. For information regarding permission, write to Scholastic Inc., Attention: Permissions Department, 557 Broadway, New York, NY 10012.

ISBN 0-439-69147-8

Copyright © 2006 by Edizioni Piemme S.p.A., Via del Carmine 5, 15033 Casale Monferrato (AL), Italia.
English translation © 2006 by Edizioni Piemme S.p.A.

GERONIMO STILTON names, characters, and related indicia are copyright, trademark, and exclusive license of Edizioni Piemme S.p.A. All rights reserved. The moral right of the author has been asserted.

Published by Scholastic Inc.

SCHOLASTIC and associated logos are trademarks and/or registered trademarks of Scholastic Inc.

Stilton is the name of a famous English cheese. It is a registered trademark of the Stilton Cheese Makers' Association. For more information, go to www.stiltoncheese.com.

Text by Geronimo Stilton
Original title: *La vita è un rodeo!*
Cover by Larry Keys
Illustrations Larry Keys, Blasco Tabasco, and Chiara Sacchi
Graphics by Merenguita Gingermouse, Moushiro Mousawa, and Gherardo DiLenna

Special thanks to Kathryn Cristaldi
Special thanks to Lidia Morson Tramontozzi
Interior design by Kay Petronio

25 24 23 22 21   14 15 16 17 18/0

Printed in the U.S.A.
First printing, January 2006

40

This book is dedicated to you.

. . . .

Write your name here

With cheesy good wishes,
Geronimo Stilton

DEAR RODENT FRIENDS...

Dear rodent friends, here it is...another whisker-licking good tale just for you, from your friend *Geronimo Stilton!*

This story is all about one of my favorite holidays, *Valentine's Day*. Yes, I guess I'm just a sappy rodent at heart.

I love all of that mushy stuff, like hearts and flowers and creamy cheese pastries.

Read on to learn all about...

...the story of *Valentine's Day!*

THE BEST
PARTY YET!

CHEESECAKE! It was February 13, and I was so excited. The next day was **Valentine's Day!** Do you like Valentine's Day? I do. Every year I throw a big party for all my **friends**. And this year was going to be the best one yet.

How Did Valentine's Day Begin?

February 14 is dedicated to all people who love one another: friends, family, parents, and sweethearts. It's a special occasion to express our feelings by giving a gift of chocolate, a poem, a flower, or…a smile!

IT'S A VERY OLD HOLIDAY

On February 14, the ancient Romans celebrated the goddess Juno, wife of the god Jupiter, and protector of women and married couples. On February 15, the feast of Lupercalia was celebrated, in honor of the god Luperco, the arrival of spring, and the fertility of the earth and animals. In the fifth century A.D., these feasts were both abolished, and February 14 became the day of Saint Valentine, the patron saint of lovers.

THE STORY OF SAINT VALENTINE

Valentine was the bishop of Terni, Italy. He was imprisoned, and then beheaded by the Roman Emperor Claudius II in A.D. 269. There are many stories in Valentine's life that show why he became the patron saint of people who love one another. This is one of them.

After school, many children went to play in Valentine's garden. One day, Valentine heard a young couple arguing there. He gave them a beautiful rose and prayed that their love would be eternal. The two made up immediately and asked Valentine to officiate at their wedding!

The invitations...

...colored streamers...

I had sent out more than one hundred *invitations* to my special friends and relatives. I had decorated my house with red streamers. I had ordered a heart-shaped cheesecake from Squeakini's, the best bakery in the city. I had even hired a **band!**

That night, I went to bed with a **smile** on my snout. I dreamed I was nibbling cheesecake at my

...the cake...

...the band!

perfectly planned, perfectly **ORGANIZED**,
fabumouse *Valentine's Day* party.

I am so happy...I am so happy...

I am so happy...I am so happy...ZZZZZZZZZZZZZZZZZZ

10:00 A.M.

I FORGOT TO SET THE ALARM CLOCK!

I woke up lazily the next morning. The SUN was already shining outside.

"Oh, what a perfect day for my Valentine's Day party," I said, yawning.

Then I spotted the clock. It was already TEN O'CLOCK!

"RATS!" I shrieked, jumping out of bed. I was so busy planning my party, I had forgotten to set my alarm clock. Now I was late for work.

My paws hit the floor running. I raced to the bathroom.

I stepped on a bar of soap...

...skidded on the rug...

Here's something you should know about running in the bathroom: Don't do it! The bathroom is a dangerous place! First, I stepped on a wet bar of soap. I *flipped into the air* and SKIDDED across the room on the rug. I landed snout-down in a tub full of water. When I stood up, I had a rubber ducky on my head. I was spitting water like a

...landed snout-down in the bathtub...

...came up spitting water...

fountain on high speed. Then I tried to pull the stopper out of the TUB, and my tail got sucked into the drain.

"Youch!" I squeaked at the top of my lungs. "I'm too fond of my tail!"

I wrapped my tail in a bandage. Then I dragged myself out the door, sobbing,

What a terrrible way to start Valentine's Day!

...my tail got sucked into the drain...

...I ran out sobbing!

THE MAILBOX IS EMPTY!

It was eleven o'clock by the time I left the house. On the way out, I checked my mailbox. Maybe a big stack of valentines would cheer me up. After all, I had lots of friends. I knew I would get lots of cards.

But the mailbox was empty.

What was going on?

I was so upset I closed the mailbox on my paw.

"Youch!" I shrieked.

I wrapped up my paw in a bandage.

Oh, what else could go wrong today?

11:00 A.M.

12:00 P.M.

THE NEWSPAPER WAS NOT DELIVERED!

I ran to the office. Oops, I almost forgot to tell you. I run a newspaper. It is called *The Rodent's Gazette*. It is the most popular paper in New Mouse City. Usually, I love going to the office. But today, something **STRANGE** was happening. A mountain of newspapers was piled up in front of the building.

At that moment, a truck unloaded a huge stack of newspapers right on top of my head.

"**Youch!**" I yelled from under the pile. I wondered if I could sue for a permanent headache.

That's when I heard a familiar voice from the next building. "**HA-HA-HA!** Geronimo Stilton, you're such a mess of a mouse!" it cackled.

It was **Sally Ratmousen**, leaning out of her office window. Sally is my number-one enemy. She runs a terrible paper called *The Daily Rat*. Her office stands directly across from *The Rodent's Gazette*.

Sally Ratmousen **is** the editor of *The Daily Rat* and Geronimo's number-one nemesis. She'll do anything to publish the hottest and oddest news before he does!

"How did you like my **Valentine's Day** gift,

I bought the NewsExpress!

Stilton?" Sally went on. "Last night, I bought the **NewsExpress**." Then she slammed her window shut noisily. **SLAM!**

My fur stood on end. Rat-munching rattlesnakes! This was a disaster. The NewsExpress is the company that delivers my paper to rodents all over Mouse Island. Sally must have told them to **STOP** delivering *The Rodent's Gazette*.

I felt a mouse-sized headache coming on.

OH, WHAT ELSE COULD GO WRONG TODAY?

I put a bandage over the big lump on my head.

I took out my cell phone and called the NewsExpress.

"Hello? This is Stilton,

Geronimo Stilton. I am the publisher of
The Rodent's Gazette..." I began.

A gruff voice at the other end interrupted
me. "*The Rodent's Gazette*? We don't deliver
it anymore!" it hollered.

The next thing I knew, I was listening to
a dial tone. I twisted my tail up in knots.
This was **SERIOUS**. The NewsExpress was
the only company big enough to deliver
newspapers to all of Mouse Island.

There was only one thing left to do. I
called Sally. I spoke in my *sweetest* squeak.

"Um...Sally, can't we just be friends?" I
tried. "After all, we both work in
the same business."

Sally let out **an evil
laugh.** "Of course we
both work in the same
business. That's why I

Ha-ha-ha!

want to put you OUT OF BUSINESS! If no one delivers your paper, the rodents of New Mouse City will be forced to read the only paper left: mine!" she cackled.

The next thing I knew, I was listening to a dial tone.

Oh, why did Sally hate me so much? I never did anything to hurt her. Well, there was that one time I pushed her into a thornbush. But it was an accident. I tripped. Really.

You can't hate a mouse for being clumsy…can you?

1:00 P.M.

THE OFFICE IS DESERTED!

It was one o'clock. I stumbled up the stairs to *The Rodent's Gazette* and burst through the door.

"I need everyone's help! *It's an emergency!*" I yelled.

No one answered. I looked around. The office was empty.

What was going on? A cold shiver ran through my fur. Was everyone sick with a deadly flu? Did they get run over by a bus? Did a pack of scary mouse aliens whisk them away in a spaceship?

Just then, I remembered something. I had given all of my employees the day off for Valentine's Day. For a minute, I was relieved. Then I remembered all of the undelivered papers.

So what did I do next? I did what any smart, sensitive, responsible mouse would do. I put my snout down on my desk and cried enough tEARS to fill an ocean. Okay,

What was going on?

The
Rodent's Gazette
EDITORIAL OFFICES

maybe not a whole ocean. Maybe just a small lake, or a stream, or a teeny-tiny tea cup. Still, you get the picture.

I was depressed. This was the worst Valentine's Day ever!

I left the office with my tail between my legs and my head hung low.

That's when I tripped. I tumbled down the stairs.

Oh, what else could go wrong today?

"Why am I such an unlucky mouse?" I said, sighing. "It's Valentine's Day!"

A gentle voice answered me. "There is no such thing as bad luck," it said.

I shook my head. Cheese niblets! Was I hearing voices?

"We each make our own luck," the voice continued.

I broke out in a sweat. I was getting ready

to check myself into the Mad Mouse Center when I saw her. She was a CHARMING rodent with light *blue* eyes and blond fur. She was dressed like a cowmouse in white leather. Around her waist, she wore a belt with a silver heart-shaped buckle. A wide-rimmed **COWMOUSE** hat was perched on her head. Spiffy **BOOTS** adorned her feet.

"Hello. My name is Cheesy Lou Sweetsnout," she said.

Cheesy Lou Sweetsnout

First name: Cheesy Lou

Last name: Sweetsnout

Nickname: Sweetness

Place of residence: Texas

Who she is: A cowmouse from the Far West

Profession: Country music singer

What she does in her free time: Loves to ride in rodeos

What she likes the most: Little heart-shaped objects from all over the world

Her secret: She is engaged to cowmouse Toughrat McBeefy, also known as Little Bull

Her dream: To become a star in Western movies

I shook her paw. "Pleased to meet you, Miss Sweetsnout. My name is Stilton, *Geronimo Stilton*," I mumbled.

The cowmouse grinned. "Seems to me you have a problem, Gerry, dear," she said. "Why don't you tell Cheesy Lou all about it?"

Now, normally I don't like it when rodents call me Gerry. And I don't like telling other mice about my problems. But Cheesy Lou had such a sweet **SMILE**. Before I knew it, I was pouring out my **WhOLe SAD STORY** to her.

She listened carefully. Then she handed me a lace handkerchief dotted with red hearts, saying sweetly . . .

"Don't worry, Gerry.

Every problem has a solution."

2:00 P.M.

EVERY PROBLEM HAS A SOLUTION

I glanced at my watch. It was two o'clock. Half the day was gone and *The Rodent's Gazette* was still undelivered. I began to nibble on my whiskers.

Cheesy Lou calmly patted my paw. She flipped open her cell phone. Then she began barking orders into it.

"Hello? Is this **HORSESHOE RANCH?**" I heard her say. "I need one hundred horses and one hundred cowmice sent to Seventeen Swiss Cheese Center—**IMMEDIATELY!**"

She hung up with a sigh of satisfaction. "Problem solved, Gerry!" she said.

A little later, we heard the sound of hoofs

GALLOPING down the street.

Cheesy Lou stuck her snout out the window. "**LISTEN up, rodents!**" she squeaked. "I need you to deliver these copies of *The Rodent's Gazette* on the double!"

The cowmice waved their hats in the air. "**We're on it, Cheesy Lou!**" they called.

2:00 P.M.

They took off at a thundering **GALLOP**. The noise was so loud I could barely hear my own squeak.

"Do you really think they can do it?" I asked Cheesy Lou.

She was calmly filing her nails. "But of course, Gerry darling. You should try to think more positively," she drawled. "Here's a little saying my grandmother Cheery Cheeks taught me. Now repeat after me, 'Life is beautiful, the world is marvelous, and I love everyone!'"

I tried. "Ahem, Life is beautiful, the world is maddening, and I love almost everyone...." I stammered. Hmmm. I guess I had to work on it.

Cheery Cheeks Sweetsnout

Cheesy Lou's grandmother

I opened my notebook and jotted down the phrase that Cheesy Lou had taught me, so that I could practice.

I thanked Miss Sweetsnout for all of her help. Then I invited her to my Valentine's Day party.

"Well, tickle me with a catfur feather!"

Toughrat McBeefy

Cheesy Lou's fiancé

she cried. "I'd love to attend your **hoedown**. I'll bring my fiancé, Toughrat McBeefy."

She took out a picture of a very muscular mouse and *kissed* it.

3:00 P.M.

A WAVE OF FOUL-SMELLING WATER

It was already three o'clock. I walked home with Cheesy Lou by my side.

"Are you sure you don't need my help anymore, Gerry?" she asked.

We had reached my house at Eight Mouseford Lane. I smiled as I opened my front door.

"Oh, no, Miss Sweetsnout. I'm sure, but thanks for the offer . . ." I started to say. But before I could finish, a wave of foul-smelling water hit me!

"Help! Blubb! Blubb! Help!"

I gurgled.

When the wave passed, I was soaked from the ends of my whiskers to the tip of my tail.

I looked around in horror. What a disaster! The sewer pipe must have burst. My house was a mess. The rugs and sofas were sopping wet. Even my walls were dripping. And the STENCH! Oh, the STENCH!

"M-m-must get f-f-f-resh air," I choked.

Heeeeelp!

I headed for the window. On the way, I slipped and twisted my ankle.

OH, WHat else couLD go WRONg today?

I lay on the floor whimpering, while Cheesy Lou bandaged my ankle.

"Gerry, I had a feeling you still needed my help," she said. She dried a chair with a rag. Then she **LIFTED** me up and plopped me down on it.

I was amazed. I mean, I'm not a scrawny rodent. In fact, some might say I need to lay off the cheesecake for a while. How could Cheesy Lou **LIFT** a plump mouse like myself?

"Where I come from, we're all into athletics," she explained. "Yessiree, Cheesy Lou just loves lifting calves."

CALF LIFTING

$\mathcal{S}$inging happily, Cheesy Lou sprang into action. She grabbed some rags and wiped up the filthy, **SLIMY** water. She washed the sofas. She hosed down the walls. She hung out the rugs to dry. I had never seen a mouse work so fast. It was like watching a mini tornado. Yes, that Cheesy Lou had more energy in her little paw than I had in my whole body!

She filled buckets and buckets and buckets of filthy water...

...washed the sofa covers...

Finally, Cheesy Lou flung open all the windows. Fresh air filled the room.

"And now for a quick spray of my favorite perfume." She giggled. "Cream Cheese in the Summertime."

Suddenly, my entire house smelled like the most delicious cream cheese soufflé.

"Life is beautiful, the world is marvelous, and I love everyone!" Cheesy Lou squeaked. "Come on, Gerry, sing along!"

...flung open all the windows...

...finally, she sprayed her perfume!

4:00 P.M.

GALLOPING THROUGH THE STREETS OF NEW MOUSE CITY

It was four o'clock.

"Life is beautiful, the world is marvelous, and I love everyone," I repeated. Hmm. I was starting to feel better already. Maybe Cheesy Lou's grandmother was onto something.

Ringgg... Ringgg... Ringgg...

Ouch!

I'm sorry!

At that moment, the phone rang.

As I reached over to answer it, I heard a loud RIP! Rats! I had split the seam in my favorite suit jacket. Then I felt a twinge in my arm.

"Ouch!" I squeaked. I had pulled a muscle in my paw. I knew I shouldn't have dropped out of that Weight Lifting for Wimps class at Rats La Lanne.

"Geronimo Stilton," I grumbled into the phone.

It was the baker. He said he couldn't deliver my big Valentine's Day order. I would have to pick it up. I sighed miserably.

Cheesy Lou put my

Er...OK...

PULLED paw in a **SLING**. I headed for my car. It wouldn't start. I tried to call a taxi, but there were none, of course. It was *Valentine's Day!*

I began to sob like a newborn mouse. **Oh, what else could go wrong today?**

Before I could **find out**, Cheesy Lou let out a high-pitched **WHISTLE**. Seconds later, a black horse came galloping down the road.

Cheesy Lou plunked me into the saddle.

"Pull on the right rein to turn right, the left rein to turn left, and both reins to stop," she explained. "And above all, **KEEP CALM**. Whatever you do, don't act scared. If the horse smells your **fear**, no one will be able to control him!"

I felt faint. I felt sick. I felt the horse take off when Cheesy Lou screeched, "**Off you go!**"

The horse galloped all the way to Squeakini's.

"My order, pleeeease!" I yelled to the baker as we burst through the door. He tossed me three enormouse boxes.

"*Send me the bill!*" I screeched as we sped away.

Heeeeelp!

The horse galloped back to my house. He flung me out of the saddle. Then he took off.

OH, WELL. I guess you get what you pay for. And the ride was free.

I was sore all over. Luckily, the pastry boxes were safe. I headed for the kitchen to put them in the refrigerator. Just then, a **ghostly figure** leaped out at me.

"**Help!**" I shrieked. "Don't hurt me!" The boxes shook in my paws.

"Oh, **GERONIMOID**, don't be such a **scaredy** mouse," the figure smirked. I blinked. It wasn't a ghost after all. It was my cousin Trap! He was dressed in a white sheet. In his paw, he held a bow and arrow.

"What do you think of my *Cupid* costume, Cousinkins?" Trap chuckled. Did I mention that my cousin is the biggest pest on the planet?

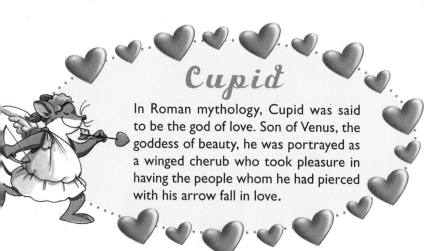

Cupid

In Roman mythology, Cupid was said to be the god of love. Son of Venus, the goddess of beauty, he was portrayed as a winged cherub who took pleasure in having the people whom he had pierced with his arrow fall in love.

5:00 P.M.
OOPS!

My whiskers were twitching. My paws were shaking. My nerves were shot. I put the pastry boxes carefully down on the table and sank into a chair. Cheesy Lou brought me a cup of **HOT COCOA**. Do you like cocoa? I do. It's so warm and yummy and soothing. I closed my eyes. Ah, I was finally starting to relax.

Then I heard a noise: **SᴘLAᴛ!** "Oops," my cousin's voice mumbled.

My eyes snapped open. "**vooooooooooo!**" I shrieked. Trap had sat on the boxes from Squeakini's.

"My mini gourmet pizzas, my pastries, my heart-shaped cheesecake!" I sobbed.

5:00 P.M.

SPLAT!

I was so upset that I didn't see the icing on the floor. I slipped. I knocked over my aunt Ratsy's *priceless* antique vase. It SHATTERED into pieces. I landed next to it on the floor. Right at that moment, Cheesy Lou swung open the door. It hit me smack in the snout.

Little butterflies danced before my eyes. "Pretty...pretty..." I babbled.

Then I fainted.

When I opened my eyes, the first thing I saw was Trap. He was *LICKING* his whiskers. "Love the pastries, Gerry Berry," he squeaked with his mouth full. "You know, they're still good even

BOOM!

CRASH!

BANG!

though they're **squished**."

Steam rose from my ears. "I can't serve squished pastries!" I **SCREAMED**.

OH, what else could go wrong today?

Meanwhile, Cheesy Lou was very busy bandaging my **black eye**. "Sorry I hit you with the door," she apologized. "But don't you worry about a thing, darling. Cheesy Lou will fix **everything**."

Cheesy Lou picked up the phone and **shouted** into it. "That's right, I need **100** pounds of flour, **16** pounds of sugar, **24** pounds of butter, and **130** eggs sent over to Eight Mouseford Lane...on the double!" she ordered.

A few minutes later,

three big rodents **GALLOPED** up on horses with the delivery.

Cheesy Lou began measuring and mixing and baking. I should have guessed she would be a *whirlwind* in the kitchen. That mouse was good at everything. I wouldn't be surprised if she was a concert pianist and an Olympic ice dancer, too! Still, I had no idea what she was so busy making.

"Um, can I help, Cheesy Lou?" I asked, watching her fill a pan with some type of batter.

"No, thanks, Gerry," she smiled. "You just **relax**. As for you, Trap, I'd like you to be my *taste-tester*."

My cousin was so **excited** that he could barely keep his paws on the ground. Besides annoying me, that mouse's favorite thing to do is eat!

A little while later, Cheesy Lou pulled an enormouse pan out of the oven. It was a delicious-looking cake shaped like a heart.

Trap licked his whiskers. He looked happier than a mouse in a cheesecake factory.

BZZZT!

It was six o'clock. I was thrilled with Cheesy Lou's cake. It was a work of art. Now I had dessert, but **what** would I feed my guests for dinner?

Just then, I heard Trap whispering into his cell phone. He was mumbling something about **tomatoes** and **mozzarella** and **flour**. I guess my cousin liked talking about food as much as he liked eating it.

I was still **worrying** about my dinner party when I heard a strange buzzing sound.

It seemed to be coming from the heart-shaped mini lights I had hung as DECORATIONS. They looked so pretty.

I hit the switch to TURN them on. BZZZT! I was ZAPPED with an ELECTRIC SHOCK! My whole body shook. My fur stood on end. I lit up like my aunt Ratilda's Christmas tree. She always overdoes it with the lights . . . but that's another story.

Suddenly, the whole house went **DARK, VERY DARK, VERY VERY DARK . . .**

Cheese niblets! A fuse must have BLOWN. Do you know what a fuse is? It helps run the electricity in your house.

Just then, a TINY LIGHT appeared behind me. It was Cheesy Lou. She held a flashlight in her paw. "Relax, Gerry, I'll take care of it," she said. "I'll check out the fuse

Ouuuch!

box in your basement. But you really should be careful, darling. **ELECTRICITY CAN BE MORE DANGEROUS THAN AN ANGRY COW!**"

She quickly bandaged my paw. I was still shaking.

Oh, what else could go wrong today?

I'll take care of it!

I followed Cheesy Lou down to the basement. A few minutes later, the lights blinked back on.

"All fixed," grinned Cheesy Lou.

I was amazed. Was there anything Cheesy Lou couldn't do?

"It's fun to learn new things, "Cheesy Lou said. "I learned all about fixing ELECTRICAL PROBLEMS from my grandfather Buzzy. Yep, he sure taught me how to light up a room."

BUZZY SWEETSNOUT
CHEESY LOU'S GRANDFATHER

NOBODY LOVES ME

It was seven o'clock, party time. But no one knocked on my door. Tears filled my eyes. I was all alone.

Oh, what a rotten, awful day!

"Nobody loves me," I sobbed. "Nobody wants to come to my PARTY."

Before long, the lights went out again. "Now what?" I whined.

OH, WHAT ELSE COULD GO WRONG today?

Suddenly, a flickering light appeared in the darkness. Uh-oh! I gulped. Was it a ghost carrying a candle? I've heard some ghosts are afraid of the dark.

"C-ch-ch-cheesy Lou?" I squeaked. "T-t-t-rap?" No one answered. Then, one by one, more flickering candles began to light up the . More ghosts? My heart hammered under my fur.

"D-d-on't hurt me," I stammered. "I come in p-p-peace."

Just then, I took a good look at the faces surrounding me. No, they weren't ghost faces. They were all of my *friends*!

"Happy Valentine's Day,

Geronimo!"

they shouted.

Happy Valentine's Day! Happy Valentine's Day! Happy Valentine's Day!

Happy Valentine's Day! Happy

Happy Valentine's Day! Happy Valentine's Day! Happy Valentine's Day!

"GERONIMO,

WE ALL LOVE YOU!"

8:00 P.M.
A LITTLE SURPRISE

I was shocked!

"But what...? But how...? But why...?" I babbled.

My friend **HERCULE POIRAT** jumped up from behind the sofa. "We were trying to organize a little surprise for you, Stilton," he beamed. "What do you think?"

I was so touched I couldn't even squeak. I felt like the richest mouse in the world. Friendship really is a TREASURE.

Right then, my cousin Trap came in pushing a wheelbarrow. It was filled with Valentine's hearts and

BOXES and *flowers*. "Special delivery, Geronimoid," he announced.

Tears sprang to my eyes. Partly because I was so happy. And partly because Trap had run over my paw with the wheelbarrow.

Ouch!

Happy Valentine's Day!

I reached into the wheelbarrow and pulled out a card addressed to **UNCLE GERONIMO**. It was a poem from my *favorite* nephew, Benjamin.

I gave him a **BIG** hug. "This is the **BEST GIFT** I have ever received!" I squeaked.

FOR UNCLE GERONIMO

You are the best uncle ever
You are so very clever,
I love you so
More than you know
I'll love you
forever and ever!

Benjamin

A GIANT PIZZA

I was still thinking about Benjamin's poem when I heard someone whining. It was my **GRANDFATHER WILLIAM**. I wasn't surprised. Grandfather William was always grumbling about something. *"I thought you were having pizza at this party,"* he complained.

Before I could reply, my cousin **Trap** grabbed me by the paw. He dragged me into the kitchen.

"What now?" I groaned. Had Trap eaten all of Cheesy Lou's cake? Had he set my toaster oven on fire?

I closed my eyes, expecting the worst. But when I opened them, I saw the

most beautiful, delicious sight. It was a super-mega-huge pizza in the shape of a heart!

"TA-DA!" Trap shouted. "What do you think, Gerrykins? Can I make a pizza or what?"

He cut a **giant** slice of the pizza. Then everyone cheered as my cousin devoured the whole thing in two bites.

Ta-da!

How Pizza Was Invented

Thousands of years ago, the Assyrians and the Babylonians made a kind of pizza with oat flour and water. It was only in the 1700s that pizza as we know it was born. The people of Naples, Italy, invented it, and it became very popular there. In 1889, King Umberto I and Queen Margherita of Italy went to Naples and tasted a pizza topped with tomatoes and mozzarella cheese. The queen liked it so much that from then on, that kind of pizza was called "Pizza Margherita." In the early 1900s, immigrant Neapolitans brought pizza with them to all different parts of the world.

Trap! Trap! Trap! Trap!

9:00 P.M.

WHERE'S THE MUSIC?

It was nine o'clock. There was a message blinking on my phone.

Uh-oh. Something told me it wasn't good news. Had I forgotten to return my library books? Did my plants need water down at *The Rodent's Gazette*?

NO, IT WAS THE BAND. THEY'D MISSED THE PLANE. NOW THEY WOULD MISS MY PARTY.

I covered my eyes with my paw. Oh, why did I have such rotten luck? "Where am I going to find a BAND at nine o'clock on Valentine's Day?" I cried.

Just then, Cheesy Lou pulled out a **business card**. She waved it under my snout. "Today must be your lucky day, Gerry darling." She chuckled.

I read the card. It said, "Cheesy Lou Sweetsnout: Professional Country Music Singer."

My jaw hit the ground. I don't know why I was SURPRISED. That Cheesy Lou had more talents than a veteran circus rat.

"You're a professional singer?" I asked.

COUNTRY MUSIC

This type of music is rooted in the folk traditions of the British Isles, and became popular in the western and southern United States. It often features fiddles, banjos, and guitars. Today, country songs are usually about love, family, friendship, nature, and memories.

Cheesy Lou was already making a phone call. "GIRLS! Come on over to Eight Mouseford Lane. We've got a gig!" she squeaked.

A few minutes later, two *charming* rodents appeared at the door.

Hi, friends!

I'm Cheesy Lee!

And I'm Cheesy Lynn!

CHEESY LEE played the guitar. Cheesy Lynn played the banjo. And Cheesy Lou played the fiddle. It was a paw-stomping country music concert!

The band even taught everyone how to _LINE DANCE_. Well, not everyone. I stepped on my tail so many times that I eventually decided to just watch. Did I mention I'm a little on the **CLUMSY** side?

LINE DANCE

One famous country dance is the line dance. There are many different types of line dances, but here's a simple one to start with. Everyone get in a line and follow these steps!

1

Bring your feet together

2

Bring your right foot out to the side and then together

3

Bring your right foot forward, tap your heel and then together

4

Bring your left foot out to the side and then together

5

Bring your left foot forward, tap your heel and then together

6

Bring your right foot forward, tap your toe and then together

7

Put your left foot behind you, tap your toe and then together

8

Put your right foot behind you, tap your toe and then together

9 **10**

Bring your right foot forward, cross it over to your left foot and turn a quarter turn. Repeat from the beginning

10:00 P.M.
A HORSE IN MY LIVING ROOM?

It was ten o'clock.

The party was in full swing. Rodents were talking and laughing and eating. I sat on the sofa happily watching my **guests**. I saw Trap stuffing his face with cake. I saw Benjamin dancing with his friend Nibblette. I saw an enormouse white horse galloping through my open window. **Rat-Munching Rattlesnakes!** What was a horse doing in my living room?

On the horse's back was a rodent with frightening muscles. "Pleased to meet you, Gerry," the mouse drawled. "I'm **TOUGHRAT McBEEFY**, Cheesy Lou's fiancé. Thanks for

10:00 P.M.

INVITING me to your party." He smiled and shook my paw.

Now, normally, I have a rule: no horses in the living room. But Toughrat seemed like a friendly kind of rodent. Plus, his grip nearly broke every bone in my paw. I didn't want to think about what he could do to me if he got angry.

Thanks for the invite!

I watched as Toughrat lassoed himself a piece of cake and a glass of **ORANGE JUICE**. Meanwhile, his **HORSE** was munching away at my houseplant.

A horse in my living room... I thought to myself.

OH, WHAT ELSE COULD GO WRONG TODAY?

11:00 P.M.
DING-DONG!

It was eleven o'clock. The doorbell rang.

Ding-dong!

Who could it be? All of my friends had already arrived.

"Who is it?" I asked before opening the door.

"**Open up, Stilton!**" a familiar voice **BARKED**. I opened the door.

Holey cheese! It was my worst enemy, Sally Ratmousen.

"Uh, hello, Sally," I squeaked in surprise.

She nodded. "Listen, Stilton," she said. "I've been thinking. Maybe the NewsExpress should keep delivering your paper. After all,

every mouse knows my paper is better than the *The Rodent's Gazette*, anyway."

I was shocked. Sally Ratmousen never does anything nice. Even her mother says so. "What great news! Thanks, Sally! That's amazing! That's wonderful! That's…" I babbled.

Sally put her paw in the air. "Enough with the chitchat, Stilton. I need to ask you something," she said.

I gulped. I should have known there was a catch. What did Sally want now? My money? My precious set of *Encyclopedia Ratannica*? My vital organs?

But I was wrong. All Sally wanted was an invitation. That's right, my worst enemy wanted to come to my Valentine's Day party!

What do you think I did? Of course, I invited her inside. One thing you should know about me: I, *Geronimo Stilton,* am a gentlemouse. I never hold a **GRUDGE**. And everyone knows Valentine's Day is a day to show your *love* toward others.

I gave Sally a box of chocolate Cheesy Chews. She gobbled them down in minutes. No, Sally Ratmousen wasn't the nicest mouse on the block. But I guess she could still be my friend. Now, if I could just teach her to chew with her mouth closed....

Some of Geronimo Stilton's Friends

THEA
Geronimo's sister and special correspondent to *The Rodent's Gazette*

CREEPELLA
Director and expert in special effects; has a weakness for Geronimo

AUNT SWEETFUR
Geronimo's favorite aunt; always gives him good advice

TRAP
Geronimo's prankster cousin, who always tries to get Geronimo to loosen up

GRANDFATHER WILLIAM
William Shortpaws, aka Cheap Mouse Willy; founder of *The Rodent's Gazette*

HERCULE POIRAT
Geronimo's best friend since nursery school; an investigator, always sticks his nose into everybody's business

TINA SPICYTAIL
Grandfather William's housekeeper; Tina is a loud mouse, but an excellent cook

SHIF T. PAWS
Geronimo's excellent business manager

BENJAMIN
Geronimo's nephew; dreams of becoming a journalist

MIDNIGHT

AN ENDLESS SUPPLY OF CHEESE

It was midnight. My guests were getting ready to go home.

"Wait, everyone! I have a great idea!" Pinky Pick called. Do you know Pinky? She is my young editorial assistant. She's very creative!

Pinky gave everyone a piece of paper. "Let's each write a Valentine's Day wish and attach it to a BALLOON. Then we can send our wishes up into the sky," she explained.

PINKY PICK
Young journalist at The Rodent's Gazette; is an expert on what's hot for young mouselets

Pinky Pick's advice: Roll up your paper before attaching it to the balloon.

SO MANY COLORED BALLOONS!
IT'S A GOOD IDEA TO HAVE DIFFERENT
COLORED BALLOONS . . .

...BECAUSE EACH ONE OF US IS DIFFERENT!

I wish for world peace, I wrote.

I wish for love and happiness for all rodents, Benjamin wrote.

I wish for an endless supply of cheese, Trap wrote.

We stood back and watched our balloons sail **INTO THE SKY**. Purple, yellow, orange, pink…each balloon carried our Valentine's Day wishes up to the clouds. Holey cheese! *What a magical sight.*

I thought about how amazing it would be if our wishes really did come true. The world would be such a wonderful, peaceful place. Every rodent would find **love** and **happiness**. And, oh, yes, there would always be lots and lots of cheese!

Happy Valentine's Day!

Cheesy Lou Sweetsnout's

How to Organize a Valentine's Day Party

Guide

How to Decorate with Paper Streamers

You can make decorative streamers out of anything — old newspapers, magazines, etc. Hang them on walls, doors, or even from the ceiling. Here's how:

Heart-Shaped Streamers

What you need: an old newspaper, red felt-tip pen, scissors, sticky tape.

1. Cut a long, rectangular strip from a sheet of newspaper. Fold it like a fan.

2. On the top rectangle, draw a heart with the pen.

3. Cut along the drawing with scissors.

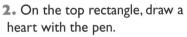

4. Open the streamer and place a little piece of sticky tape at each end. Now stick your heart streamer wherever you'd like.

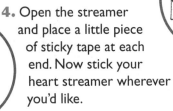

STREAMERS WITH FLOWERS

What you need: Old magazines, red tissue paper, scissors, pencil, glue, and sticky tape.

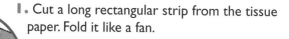

1. Cut a long rectangular strip from the tissue paper. Fold it like a fan.

2. With the pencil, draw a circle on the top sheet.

3. Cut along the drawing with scissors.

4. Find some pictures of flowers in old magazines and cut them out with the scissors.

5. Open the streamer and glue the flowers that were cut from the magazines on every circle.

6. Put a piece of sticky tape on each end. Now stick it up wherever you like.

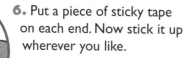

Sweet Thoughts!

Learn how to prepare desserts and mini pizzas for your friends. They'll lick their whiskers with delight!

Friendship Sweets

What you need: two sponge cakes, blueberry or raspberry jam, orange marmalade, shelled almonds, chocolate pieces, cookie cutter in the shape of a heart.

1. Cut as many hearts from the sponge cake with the heart-shaped cookie cutter as you can.

2. Spread the orange marmalade on some of the hearts and on the others, the blueberry or raspberry jam.

3. Top the blueberry or raspberry jam with almond pieces, and the orange marmalade with chocolate bits.

Mini Heart Pizzas

What you need: bread dough; tomato sauce; shredded cheese; sliced red, yellow, and green roasted peppers; two cookie cutters (the bigger of the two for the mini pizzas, and the smaller one for the peppers); flour; rolling pin.

1. Put a little flour on the table and flatten the bread dough with the rolling pin.

2. With the bigger cookie cutter, cut hearts out of the dough.

3. Top each heart with tomato sauce, and garnish with cheese.

4. With the smaller cookie cutter, cut out hearts from the pepper slices and place one on top of each mini pizza.

5. Ask an adult for help cooking the mini pizzas. Preheat the oven to 350°F. Bake for about 20 minutes or until the crust is golden brown and the cheese is bubbling.

You can also make heart-shaped fried eggs by cooking the egg inside one of the heart-shaped cookie cutters!

GAMES MOUSIES PLAY

The best part of a party is playing happily together. Suggest the following games to your friends. Then have a fabumouse time!

PASS THE HEART

What you need: two pillows (it would be nice if you could find heart-shaped ones).

To form two teams, put as many slips of paper as there are players inside a paper bag. On one half of the slips of paper, draw a red heart. On the other half, draw a black heart. Mix the slips of paper in the bag, and ask each player to pull out a slip. Once everyone has picked a slip of paper, two teams will emerge: one with red hearts, the other with black hearts.

Each team forms a line. The first player on each line puts the pillow between his knees and passes it to the next member of the team, who takes it, without using his hands, and puts it between his knees. He passes it on to the next player on his team, and so on, until the last player has the pillow between his knees. The first team to get their pillow to the end of the line wins!

PAIR BY PAIR

Split into two even teams.

The first player on Team A thinks of a pair. It could be a pair of people, like Cinderella and Prince Charming, Beauty and the Beast, Batman and Robin, or Barbie and Ken. Or it could be a pair of things, like milk and cookies, fork and knife, sun and moon, or peanut butter and jelly.

That player asks the other team to complete the pair. For example, if Team A says, "Cinderella," Team B answers, "Prince Charming." Team A and Team B should take turns until each person has thought of a pair.

GIVE THE GIFT OF A SMILE!

The most precious gifts are those you make yourself. They show your friends and relatives that you're always thinking about them.

EXTRAORDINARY CARDS

What you need: red, white, and pink construction paper; scissors; black marker; glue; yarn.

I. Make a heart using the red construction paper, a smaller one with the pink paper, and three very small ones with the white construction paper. Cut them out with the scissors.

2. Glue the red and pink hearts together. They will be the body and the head of the mouse.

3. Glue a white heart where the nose would be, and the other two where the ears would be.

4. With the marker, draw the eyes. Make the whiskers and tail by cutting some yarn and gluing it in the appropriate places.

5. Write something on the inside of your card.

HAPPY VALENTINE'S DAY

AN EXTRAORDIMOUSY FRIEND!
A VERY SPECIAL FLOWER

What you need: a white paper cup; red markers; white crayons; pebbles; pencil; red and green construction paper; a green straw; sticky tape; a photo; glue; scissors.

1. Color the paper cup with the red marker.

2. Let it dry well, then write "Happy Valentine's Day!" on it with the white marker.

3. Fill the container with pebbles.

4. Draw two leaves on the green construction paper; draw a heart on the red construction paper. Cut them out with the scissors.

5. Glue your photo in the center of the heart.

6. Attach the leaves and the heart to the green plastic stick, using the sticky tape. It should look like a flower.

7. Stick the "flower" in the container with the pebbles and give it to a special person.

WRITE A VALENTINE POEM

A poem is truly a very special gift that lets you express how you really feel. To find inspiration, look in your heart and think about your feelings: happiness, friendship, love, and all the rest.

Start playing with the sound of the words, and try writing words that rhyme. Rhymes are phrases or sentences whose last word has the same sound as the sentence that comes before or after. Here are some rhyming ideas that will help you to write your valentine poem. The words are grouped according to how they sound. Enjoy!

RHYMING WORDS

Ball: Tall, Small, Wall, Call

Cheese: Please, Knees, Sneeze, Bees

Cone: Tone, Groan, Phone

Friend: End, Send, Bend

Gift: Lift, Swift, Drift

Heart: Part, Start, Smart, Cart, Mart

Kite: Night, Fright, Right, Bite

Love: Above, Dove, Of, Glove, Shove

Mouse: House, Douse, Blouse

Rat: Cat, Bat, Sat, Flat, Pat, Mat

Ring: Sing, Bring, Sting, Thing

School: Rule, Tool, Pool, Cool

Sky: Pie, Eye, Fly, High, Try, Buy, Tie

Stars: Mars, Cars, Jars

Sun: Fun, Done, Ton, One

Treasure: Measure, Pleasure

You are such a special friend
Our friendship will never end
When I'm with you, I have so much fun
Let's play all day in the bright, warm sun.

Dear rodent friends,
I hope you like this silly
Valentine's Day poem
I wrote just for you.

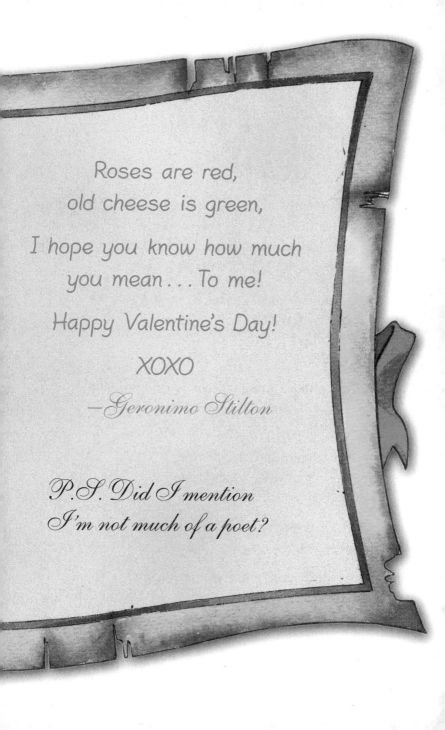

Roses are red,
old cheese is green,

I hope you know how much
you mean... To me!

Happy Valentine's Day!

XOXO

—Geronimo Stilton

P.S. Did I mention
I'm not much of a poet?

Geronimo's Joke Contest Winners!

Special thanks to all my mouse friends who sent me jokes! All the jokes were absolutely hilari-mouse. In fact, I laughed so hard, I almost broke my funny bone! Here are some of my favorites.

If a mouse lost his tail, where would he go to get a new one?
A re-tail store!
From Flannery in Washington State

When should a mouse carry an umbrella?
When it's raining cats and dogs!
From Caleb in Maryland

What animal is a tattletale?
A pig. It always squeals on you!
From Emily in Ohio

What's a mouse's favorite state?
Swissconsin!

Why do rodents like earthquakes?
Because they like to shake, rattle, and MOLE.
From Amanda in California

What's the tallest building in the world?
The library, of course! It has the most stories.

What do you call something easy to chew?
A ch-easy chew!

From Darianne in New Hampshire

What martial art does Geronimo Stilton like to practice?
Tai Cheese!

From Ryan in Texas

What happens to a cat when it eats a lemon?
It turns into a sourpuss!

From Tiffany in Florida

How do you make a tissue dance?
You put a little boogie in it.

From Zachery in New Jersey

What do you call a group of mice in disguise?
A mouse-querade party!

From the Freed family in Michigan

How does a mouse feel after a shower?
Squeaky clean!

From Ian in Washington State

What do you call a mouse that's the size of an elephant?
Enor-mouse!

From Parker

Who was the first cat to come to America?
Christo-fur Colum-puss!

From Nora in Virginia

What's black and white and red all over?
The Rodent's Gazette! It's READ all over.

ABOUT THE AUTHOR

Born in New Mouse City, Mouse Island, Geronimo Stilton is Rattus Emeritus of Mousomorphic Literature and of Neo-Ratonic Comparative Philosophy. For the past twenty years, he has been running *The Rodent's Gazette*, New Mouse City's most widely read daily newspaper.

Stilton was awarded the Ratitzer Prize for his scoop on *The Curse of the Cheese Pyramid*. He has also received the Andersen 2000 Prize for Personality of the Year. One of his best-sellers won the 2002 eBook Award for world's best ratlings' electronic book. His works have been published all over the globe.

In his spare time, Mr. Stilton collects antique cheese rinds and plays golf. But what he most enjoys is telling stories to his nephew Benjamin.

THE RODENT'S GAZETTE

1. **Main Entrance**
2. **Printing presses (where the books and newspaper are printed)**
3. **Accounts department**
4. **Editorial room (where the editors, illustrators, and designers work)**
5. **Geronimo Stilton's office**
6. **Storage space for Geronimo's books**

Don't miss any of my other fabumouse adventures

#1 Lost Treasure of the Emerald Eye

#2 The Curse of the Cheese Pyramid

#3 Cat and Mouse in a Haunted House

#4 I'm Too Fond of My Fur!

#5 Four Mice Deep in the Jungle

#6 Paws Off, Cheddarface!

#7 Red Pizzas for a Blue Count

#8 Attack of the Bandit Cat

#9 A Fabumouse Vacation for Geronimo

#10 All Because of a Cup of Coffee

#11 It's Halloween, You 'Fraidy Mouse!

#12 Merry Christmas, Geronimo

The Phantom the Subway

#14 The Temple of the Ruby of Fire

#15 The Mona Mousa Code

#16 A Cheese-Colored Camper

7 Watch Your iskers, Stilton

#18 Shipwreck on the Pirate Islands

#19 My Name Is Stilton, Geronimo Stilton

#20 Surf's Up, Geronimo!

and coming soon

!1 The Wild, Wild West

#22 The Secret of Cacklefur Castle

A Christmas Tale

#24 Field Trip to Niagara Falls

Map of New Mouse City

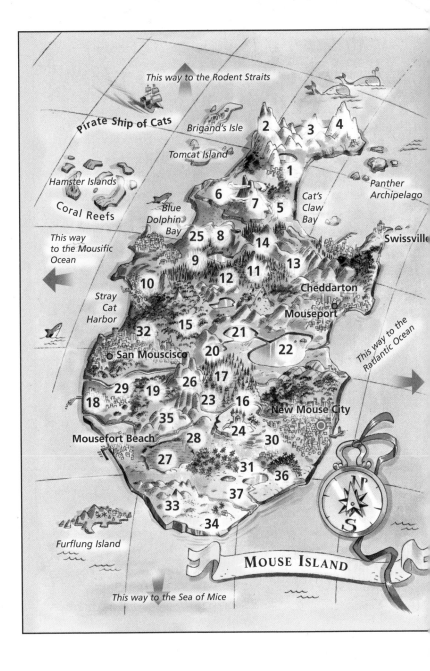

Map of Mouse Island

1. Big Ice Lake
2. Frozen Fur Peak
3. Slipperyslopes Glacier
4. Coldcreeps Peak
5. Ratzikistan
6. Transratania
7. Mount Vamp
8. Roastedrat Volcano
9. Brimstone Lake
10. Poopedcat Pass
11. Stinko Peak
12. Dark Forest
13. Vain Vampires Valley
14. Goose Bumps Gorge
15. The Shadow Line Pass
16. Penny Pincher Lodge
17. Nature Reserve Park
18. Las Ratayas Marinas
19. Fossil Forest
20. Lake Lake
21. Lake Lakelake
22. Lake Lakelakelake
23. Cheddar Crag
24. Cannycat Castle
25. Valley of the Giant Sequoia
26. Cheddar Springs
27. Sulfurous Swamp
28. Old Reliable Geyser
29. Vole Vale
30. Ravingrat Ravine
31. Gnat Marshes
32. Munster Highlands
33. Mousehara Desert
34. Oasis of the Sweaty Camel
35. Cabbagehead Hill
36. Rattytrap Jungle
37. Rio Mosquito

Dear mouse friends,
Thanks for reading, and farewell
till the next book.
It'll be another whisker-licking-good
adventure, and that's a promise!

Geronimo Stilton

3 1901 03907 6601